MITCH MARNER

HOCKEY SUPERSTAR

BY ROY RATHBURN

Book design by Jake Nordby
Cover design by Jake Nordby

Photographs ©: Peter Power/AP Images, cover, 1; Claus Andersen/Getty Images Sport/Getty Images, 4, 8, 11, 14; Frank Gunn/The Canadian Press/AP Images, 6; Bruce Bennett/Getty Images Sport/Getty Images, 13, 22; Gregory Shamus/Getty Images Sport/Getty Images, 17; Adam Glanzman/Getty Images Sport/Getty Images, 19; Jeffrey T. Barnes/AP Images, 20–21; Cole Burston/The Canadian Press/AP Images, 25; Chris O'Meara/AP Images, 27, 30; Red Line Editorial, 29

Press Box Books, an imprint of Press Room Editions, Inc.

ISBN
978-1-63494-874-6 (library bound)
978-1-63494-892-0 (paperback)
978-1-63494-926-2 (epub)
978-1-63494-910-1 (hosted ebook)

Library of Congress Control Number: 2023922782

Distributed by North Star Editions, Inc.
2297 Waters Drive
Mendota Heights, MN 55120
www.northstareditions.com

Printed in the United States of America
082024

About the Author

Roy Rathburn is a retired English teacher and former hockey player, coach, and official, from northern Minnesota.

TABLE OF CONTENTS

16
WARRIOR
16
CCM

1 MARNER'S MAGIC MINUTE

Time was running out on the Toronto Maple Leafs. Less than 10 minutes remained in the game. The Leafs needed two goals to pull even with the Carolina Hurricanes. Suddenly, Mitch Marner gave the Toronto crowd some hope.

Teammate Auston Matthews spun free and found Marner with a pass. The right winger shot a perfect one-timer that the goalie had no chance of stopping. The Leafs now trailed by one. But they still had work to do.

Mitch Marner recorded 67 points in 59 games during the 2019–20 season.

Marner (16) and Auston Matthews celebrate one of Marner's goals against the Hurricanes.

Just 53 seconds later, it was Marner's turn to set up a score. He controlled a loose puck to the goalie's right. Marner kept his head up and looked for a teammate. He spotted Tyson Barrie driving toward the net. Barrie faked out the goalie and scored the tying goal.

The Leafs weren't done. Immediately after the next face-off, Marner stole the puck. He skated past two Hurricanes defenders and made his way toward the net. Marner shifted the puck from his forehand to his backhand and back again. With the goalie down on his knees, Marner fired home the game-winning goal.

The Leafs had gone from losing to winning in just 59 seconds. They went on to add another goal and won the game 8–6. With players like Marner, Leafs fans never had a reason to lose hope.

MAKING THE SCORE SHEET

Coming into the game on December 23, 2019, Mitch Marner hadn't scored at home in more than two months. But fans could almost always count on Marner to contribute in some way. He had recorded at least one assist in 11 of 15 home games that season.

BAUER
KNIGHTS
CABLE
CCM
Reebok
Reebok

2 TORONTO THROUGH AND THROUGH

Mitch Marner was born on May 5, 1997, in Markham, Ontario. While growing up near Toronto, Mitch was similar to most other kids. He loved hockey. And he loved the Maple Leafs.

Few kids end up playing for their hometown team. But early on, Mitch showed the kind of talent that made it possible for his dream to come true. As a seven-year-old, Mitch averaged nearly three goals per game.

Mitch Marner started playing for the London Knights when he was 16.

Mitch was always one of the smaller kids on the ice. But he didn't let that stop him. He used his quickness and stickhandling to avoid bigger, stronger players. As Mitch grew up, the competition got tougher. His scoring slowed down a bit. However, he learned to use his playmaking ability to help his teammates score.

At the age of 15, Mitch received a scholarship offer to play for the University of Michigan. He decided to play junior hockey for the London Knights instead. The Knights had selected him in the 2013 Ontario Hockey League (OHL) draft.

TAKING CARE OF BUSINESS

In high school, Mitch Marner was friends with future NHL player Christian Dvorak. The two boys were teammates on the London Knights. But they focused on more than just hockey. They also started their own business. It was a small café called MOD Feast. They served bagels, pizza, and more.

Mitch Marner scored 96 goals in three seasons with the London Knights.

As a member of the Knights, Mitch played alongside future National Hockey League (NHL) players Matthew Tkachuk and Max Domi. Mitch scored just 13 goals in his rookie season. But he recorded 46 assists. He finished as the runner-up for Rookie of the Year.

The next season, Mitch more than doubled his point total. He scored 44 goals and added

82 assists. His 126 points were the second-most in the OHL. Those numbers made Mitch a top prospect for the 2015 NHL Entry Draft.

Any hockey player would love to be a top-three pick in the draft. But Mitch didn't mind falling out of the top three since Toronto owned the fourth pick. The Maple Leafs used their pick on Mitch and made his childhood dream come true. He was going to play for his hometown team.

But first, he spent one more year in the OHL. The young star had another great season. And he delivered in the playoffs. Mitch led the league with 44 points and helped the Knights win the championship. The next year, he traveled up the road to play for Toronto.

Mitch Marner was one of seven OHL players taken in the first round of the 2015 NHL Entry Draft.

TORONTO
MAPLE
LEAFS

16
BAUER
TORONTO
MAPLE
LEAFS

3 ON HOME ICE

Going into the 2016–17 season, Maple Leafs fans had plenty to be excited about. The team boasted a core of promising rookies. Mitch Marner was one of them. Centers Auston Matthews and William Nylander were the others. All three players had been top draft picks. And all three brought skill and scoring to the team.

Matthews dazzled with four goals in his NHL debut. In the next game, Marner stole the show. No defenders were near

Marner celebrates scoring his first NHL goal.

ASSISTING THE COMMUNITY

As a Toronto native, Mitch Marner is passionate about helping his local community. He started the Marner Assist Foundation to raise money for all sorts of good causes. The charity has helped create opportunities for young people to play hockey. It also has many off-ice events, such as running food drives for hungry families.

Marner when a teammate hit him with a pass at center ice. The puck was a bit behind him. But Marner tapped it through his own legs and kept moving forward. Then he picked out a corner and fired the puck into the net for his first NHL goal.

That season, Marner set the Leafs rookie record for assists. Meanwhile, Matthews set the team rookie record for goals. All three rookies had 60 points or more. Three rookies on the same team hadn't reached those scoring numbers since 1981. Fans in Toronto looked forward to a bright future.

Marner's 42 assists led all NHL rookies in the 2016–17 season.

However, the 2017–18 season didn't go according to plan. Marner notched a goal on opening night. But he scored just once more over the next 33 games. Things picked up eventually, and Marner finished the season with 22 goals. But it wasn't the big step forward he'd been hoping for.

The next season, the Leafs signed free agent John Tavares. The veteran center added experience to a young team. Marner ended up playing on the same line with Tavares. They clicked right away. Marner shattered his previous career high, recording 94 total points. It had been years since a Leafs player racked up that many points in a season. In fact, Marner hadn't even been born yet when Mats Sundin tallied 94 points in 1996–97. Now Marner was making Leafs history himself.

Marner's 26 goals in the 2018–19 season were a career high for him at the time.

16
CCM
TRUE
VAUGHN
40

GOING FOR TWO

Marner did all the scoring work for the Leafs on November 3, 2016. Two weeks after scoring his first NHL goal, he scored both goals in a 2–1 win over the Buffalo Sabres. On his second goal, he used patience to work around the goalie and score on a wide-open net.

Reebok

MARNER

4 THE NEW LEAFS

After Marner's great 2018–19 season, the Maple Leafs rewarded him with a new contract. The deal would keep him in Toronto for six years. The 2019–20 season included more thrills. One exciting moment came when Marner led a third-period comeback against the Carolina Hurricanes. He also made the All-Star Game for the first time.

However, the COVID-19 pandemic put the season on hold for months. When it restarted, Toronto failed to reach

Marner scored his first career hat trick during a game in 2022.

the playoffs. The pandemic affected the next season's schedule, too. And Marner failed to build on his impressive scoring total from 2018–19.

With a full schedule in 2021–22, Marner finally got back on track. He and Matthews found success with new linemate Michael Bunting. Marner set new career highs with 35 goals and 97 points. In 2022–23, Marner upped his scoring yet again. He finished the season with 99 points and led Toronto in points for the fourth time in his career.

SWEET 16

Mitch Marner wore No. 93 in junior hockey. He chose it as a tribute to Leafs legend Doug Gilmour, who wore the same number. However, Toronto had retired Gilmour's number, so it wasn't available to Leafs players when Marner entered the NHL. Gilmour gave his permission for Marner to wear it, but he declined. Instead, Marner stuck with the No. 16 the team assigned him. He's worn it ever since.

Marner regularly uses his speed to get past defenders.

By this point, Marner's regular-season scoring was well established. But he hadn't yet made a big impact in the playoffs. Going into the 2023 playoffs, Marner had only scored six goals in 39 playoff games. And the Maple Leafs had lost in the first round every year. Some fans wondered if Marner would ever be able to perform on the NHL's biggest stage.

By 2023, the Leafs hadn't won a playoff series in 19 years. And they lost Game 1 to the Tampa Bay Lightning 7–3. It looked like another early exit was in the works. But in Game 2, Marner scored within the first minute and led his team to victory. Toronto went on to win the series in six games.

The Leafs fell to the Florida Panthers in the next round. Even so, the team was making progress. For a lifelong Leafs fan like Marner, ending the playoff losing streak meant a lot. Fans in Toronto dream that someday Marner will lead the team to a Stanley Cup championship.

Marner tallied 14 points in 11 games during the 2023 playoffs.

16
CCM
A
TRUE
HZR
PX

TIMELINE

1. **Markham, Ontario (May 5, 1997)**
   Mitch Marner is born.

2. **London, Ontario (April 6, 2013)**
   Mitch is drafted by the London Knights of the Ontario Hockey League.

3. **Sunrise, Florida (June 26, 2015)**
   Marner is drafted by his hometown Toronto Maple Leafs with the fourth pick in the NHL Entry Draft.

4. **Red Deer, Alberta (May 29, 2016)**
   Marner wins MVP honors as he leads the Knights to the 2016 Memorial Cup title.

5. **Toronto, Ontario (October 15, 2016)**
   Marner scores his first NHL goal in his home debut, helping the Leafs beat the Boston Bruins 4-1.

6. **Montreal, Quebec (April 6, 2019)**
   Marner scores his 94th and final point of the season, the most for a Leafs player since 1997.

7. **St. Louis, Missouri (January 25, 2020)**
   Marner plays in his first NHL All-Star Game.

8. **Tampa, Florida (April 29, 2023)**
   Marner and the Leafs beat the Tampa Bay Lightning to win their first playoff series in 19 years.

MAP

AT A GLANCE

Birth date: May 5, 1997

Birthplace: Markham, Ontario

Position: Right wing

Shoots: Right

Size: 6 feet (183 cm), 181 pounds (82 kg)

NHL team: Toronto Maple Leafs (2016–)

Previous team: London Knights (2013–16)

Major awards: NHL All-Star (2020, 2023), NHL All-Rookie Team (2017)

Accurate through the 2022–23 season.

GLOSSARY

assist
A pass, rebound, or deflection that results in a goal.

contract
A written agreement that keeps a player with a team for a certain amount of time.

debut
First appearance.

draft
An event that allows teams to choose new players coming into the league.

free agent
A player who can sign with any team.

junior hockey
A level of hockey in which young players can improve their skills.

line
A set of defensemen or forwards that a player typically is paired with while on the ice.

one-timer
A shot that a player takes directly from a pass without controlling the puck first.

prospect
A player that people expect to do well at a higher level.

rookie
A first-year player.

veteran
A player who has spent several years in a league.

TO LEARN MORE

Books

Berglund, Bruce. *Hockey GOATs: The Greatest Athletes of All Time*. North Mankato, MN: Capstone Press, 2024.

Hanlon, Luke. *Toronto Maple Leafs*. Mendota Heights, MN: Press Box Books, 2023.

Wiseman, Blaine. *Stanley Cup*. New York: Lightbox Learning, 2024.

More Information

To learn more about Mitch Marner, go to **pressboxbooks.com/AllAccess**.

These links are routinely monitored and updated to provide the most current information available.

INDEX